Spring Cleaning

by Pat Tornborg

Illustrated by
Nancy W. Stevenson

Featuring Jim Henson's Sesame Street Muppets

A SESAME STREET/GOLDEN PRESS BOOK
Published by Western Publishing Company, Inc.
in conjunction with Children's Television Workshop.

"Well, Ernie, it's time for spring cleaning again,"
said Bert one April morning. "Let's finish our oatmeal
and Crispy Critters and get started."

"Let's go, Bert," said Ernie, when they had finished eating. "I'll take out the trash while you tidy up the kitchen.... Boy, this can is really heavy."

By the time Ernie came back inside, Bert had washed the dishes and mopped the floor.

"Well, Bert," said Ernie, "that's one hard job that's done!"

"Ernie!" cried Bert. "Look at those footprints! And I just finished mopping this floor. Will you please clean it up while I start on the living room?"

Ernie got some scrub brushes out of the cupboard under the sink.

"Gee, this floor is a mess," he said. "I'll clean it up in a jiffy."

Just then Bert called him from the next room.

"Gangway, Bert!" said Ernie, as he whizzed into the living room on his brushes. "I might as well wash this floor, too. Gee, it sure is slippery!"

Bert frowned. "That's because I just finished waxing it, Ernie."

"What next, old buddy?"
Ernie looked around. " Shall
I take these rugs out for an
airing?"

Bert dusted the furniture and started to wash
the window. Suddenly, clouds of dust began pouring
through the open window. "Ernie," Bert yelled,
"what's going on out there?"

"I'm giving the rugs a good beating," called
Ernie, "and I'm practicing my tennis swing at the
same time. Cleaning is a breeze, Bert!"

Bert finished the window and picked up all the toys and clothes. Finally the living room was neat.

Then Ernie came back inside. "How about a hard job this time, Bert?" he asked.

"All right, Ernie. You clean out the hall closet while I tidy up the bedroom, okay?"

It didn't take Ernie long to clean out the closet.
"Bert, come see!" he called. "The hall closet looks
great now. Spring cleaning is a terrific idea."

"Good work, Ernie," said Bert. "The closet looks fine. What did you do with the stuff that was in it?"
"Turn around, Bert," said Ernie.

"Oh, no, my living room!" moaned Bert. "Ernie,
what have you done?"

"It's a shame to hide all that good stuff in
the closet, Bert, so I put it out here where everyone
can see it!" said Ernie proudly.

Bert snatched a stray sock off the doorknob and handed it to Ernie. "Find the sock that matches this one, Ernie, and put them away. I'll fix the living room again."

A little while later Bert came into the bedroom.

"What are you up to now, Ernie?" he asked. "I've cleaned this room up already."

"Look, Bert," said Ernie, "I found the other sock in the bottom of the drawer. Now I can put them both away together."

"I just don't know what to say, Ernie," said Bert.
"Oh, don't try to thank me, Bert," said Ernie, "I just did my job. What now?"
"The bathroom," said Bert. "There's not much in there you can mess up. Just wash everything."

Soon Bert heard loud splashing in the bathroom. "That's right, Ernie. Use plenty of soap and water!" he called.

"You bet, Bert," Ernie called back. "I've already used a whole bottle of bubble bath, too."

"Bubble bath?" Bert rushed to the bathroom door and saw Ernie in a tubful of suds.

"Ernie, why are you taking a bath?" he asked.

"You told me to wash everything," answered Ernie, "so I started with the most important things — Rubber Duckie and ME."

"I might as well clean the bathroom myself," said Bert crossly.

"Well, Bert, if you insist," said Ernie, "I am kind of tired. I'll fix myself a little snack and rest for a minute."

So while Ernie dozed in his cozy armchair, Bert raced around and finished cleaning the apartment.

Just as Bert fell, exhausted, into his own chair, Ernie woke up from his nap and looked around.

"Gee, Bert," he said. "The house looks great! We did a good spring cleaning job, didn't we?"

But Bert didn't answer. He was fast asleep.

ABCDEFG